Sleepy Book

Sleepy Book

by Charlotte Zolotow

pictures by Stefano Vitale

HarperCollinsPublishers

Bears
sleep
in
their
dark
caves
the long
winter
through

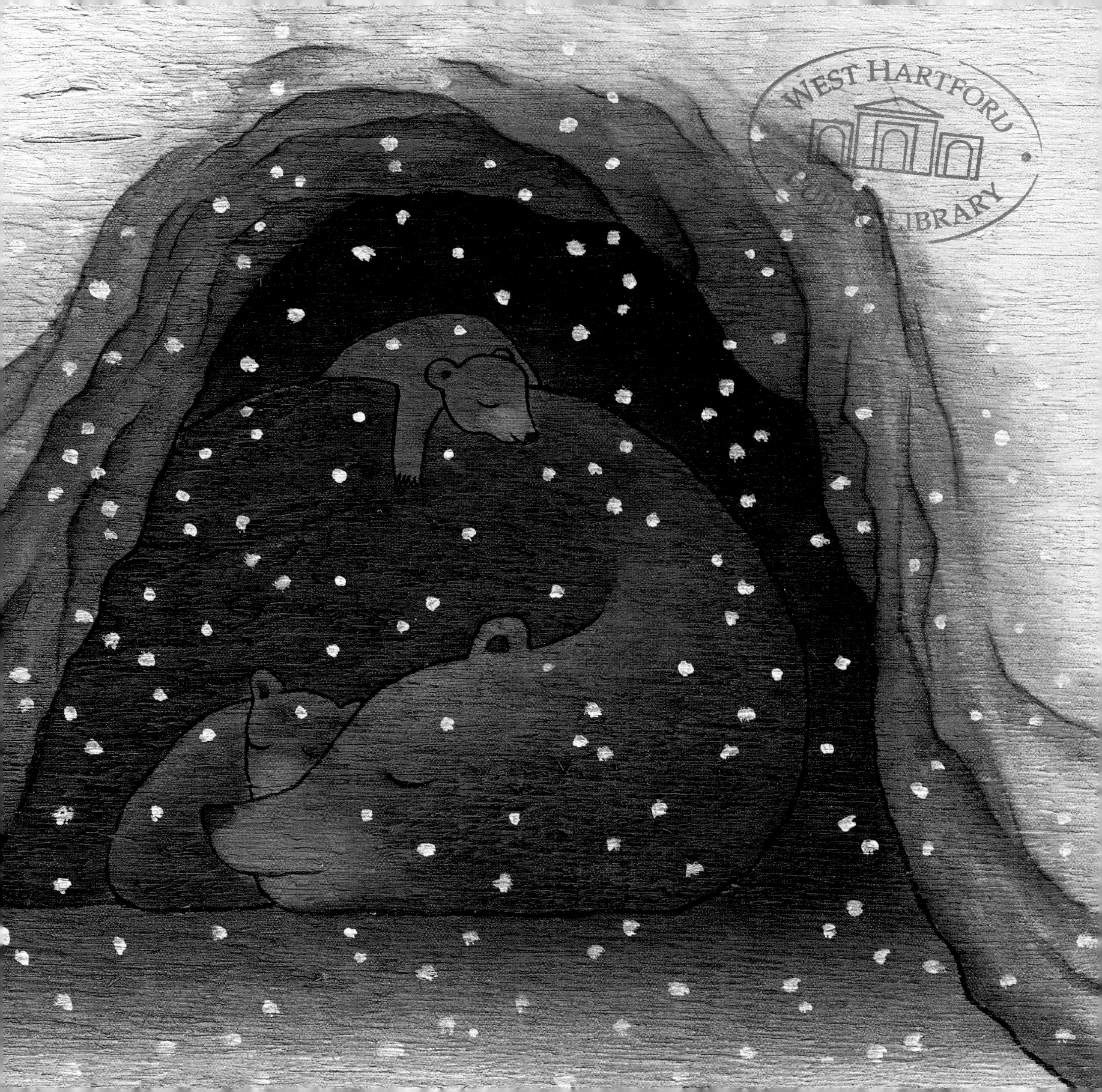

pigeons
sleep
in
a row
pressing
against
each other
for
warmth

fish sleep
among
the green
water ferns
with
their eyes
and mouths
wide
open

moths

sleep

with wings

folded together

they look like

little

white leaves

on walls

and windows

and screens

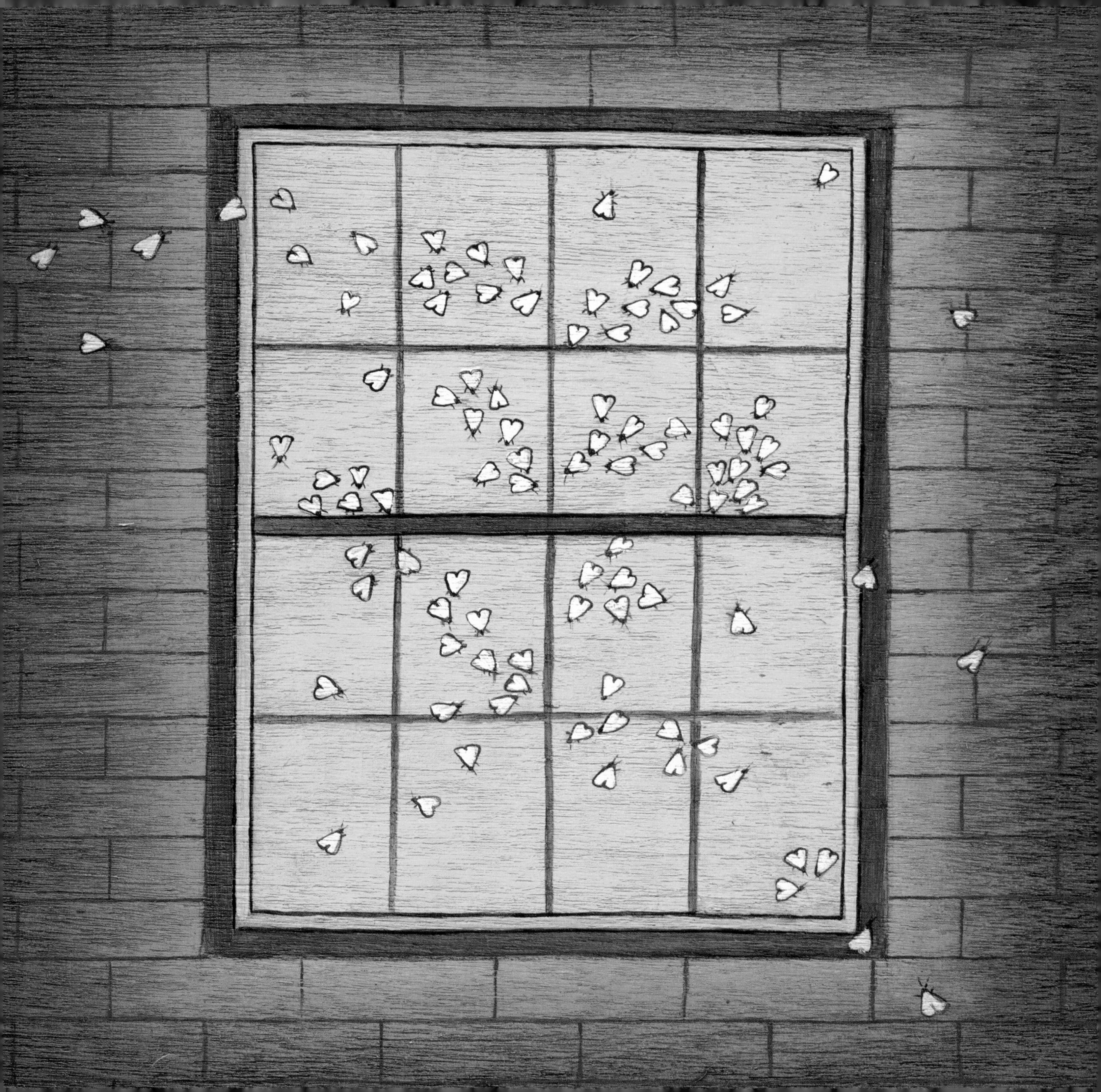

horses
sleep
standing up
in fields
and stalls
their tails
switching
to keep away
the flies

seals
sleep
with
their
flippers
flat
against
blocks of
ice

the snowy
crane
sleeps
standing
on one long
leg
like
a flower
on its
stem

crickets
sleep in
the long
meadow grass
and look
like the grass
itself—
they are
so
still

turtles
sleep inside
their
shells
and no one
would know
a turtle
was there

caterpillars
sleep in
their
silky
cocoons

spiders
when
they sleep
are like
small
ink spots
in the
middle of
their
lacy webs

kittens
sleep
in the warmest
place
they can find—
curled up
in a basket or
stretched out
purring
in the sun

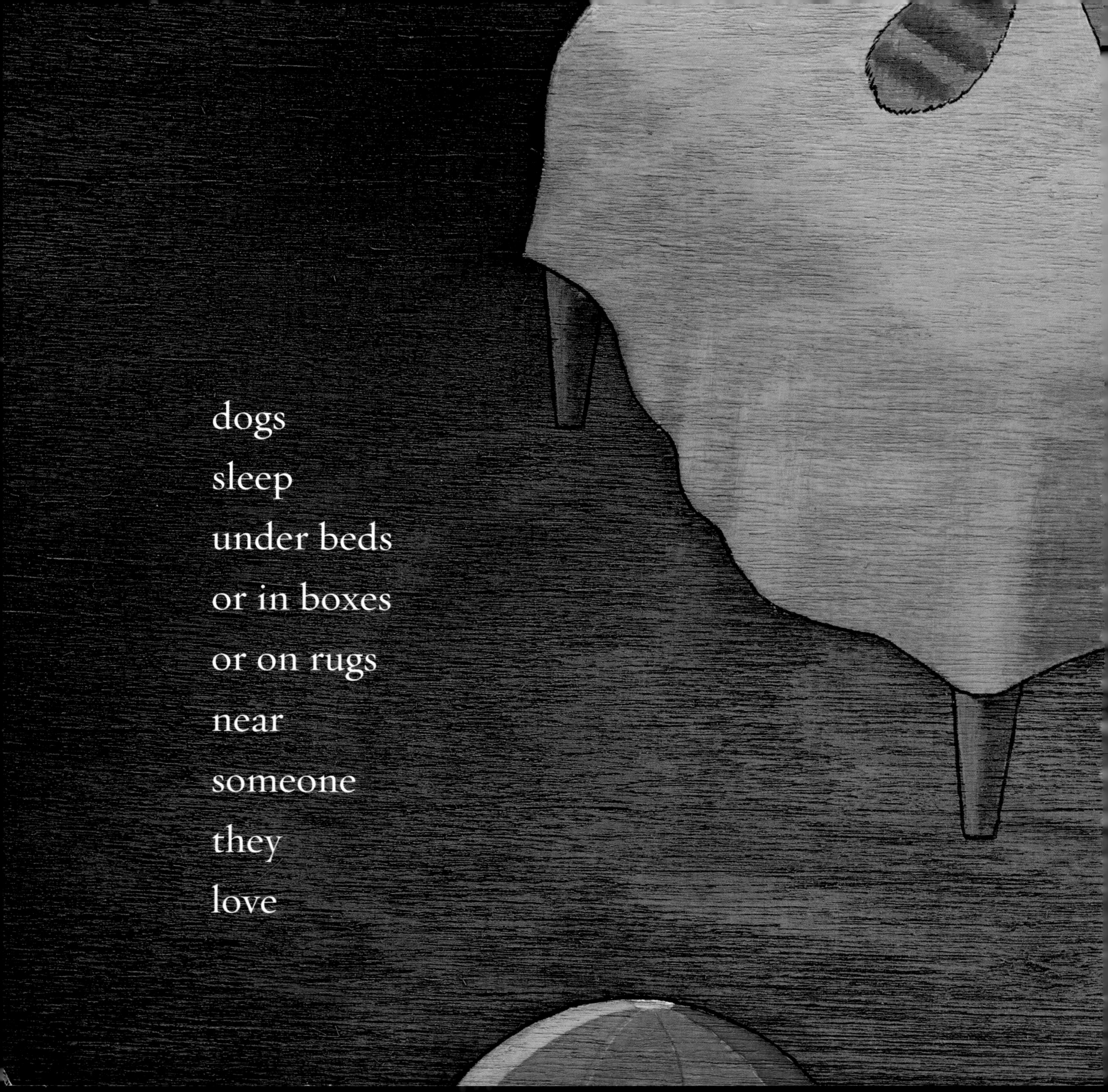

dogs
sleep
under beds
or in boxes
or on rugs
near
someone
they
love

but little boys
and girls,
when the night
comes
and the wind
whispers gently
in the trees
and the stars
sparkle and shine,
sleep
warm under
their blankets
in their
beds.

to my mother

Sleepy Book

www.harperchildrens.com

Library of Congress Cataloging-in-Publication Data
Zolotow, Charlotte.
Sleepy book / by Charlotte Zolotow ; illustrations by Stefano Vitale.
p. cm.
Originally published: 1958
ISBN 0-06-027873-0 — ISBN 0-06-027874-9 (lib. bdg.)
1. Sleep behavior in animals—Juvenile literature. [1. Animals—Sleep behavior. 2. Animals—Habits and behavior. 3. Sleep.] I. Vitale, Stefano ill. II. Title.
QL755.3 .Z66 2001
591.5'19—dc21
00-057252

Typography by Pamela Berry
2 3 4 5 6 7 8 9 10
❖
Newly Illustrated Edition